A long time ago in Congo, there was a very spoiled little boy. His dad, the King, gave him anything he wanted. He wore elegant hats, fine shirts, and gold chains and bangles. He feasted on rich meat stews, baked fish, and roasted peanuts.

The spoiled boy never even had to walk anywhere. As soon as he was tired, he would click his fingers and servants would appear to carry him around on a throne! It was a life of extreme riches, but the boy was never satisfied.

One morning, the boy was bored. He whined to his dad.

“Dad, I’m so bored. I need a kingdom of my own.”

The King could never say “no” to his boy, so instead he let him rule over all of the children in the kingdom.

The boy liked showing off very much! He would parade around before the children, and make them cheer whenever they saw him. The children had to follow the boy around, and sit still while he ate or took a nap. It was all very dull for the children.

One little girl became very annoyed with the boy's boasting and greed. As the boy feasted on yams one day, she shouted at him.

"There is at least one thing you can never have," she shouted.

The boy was very angry.

"What can I not have?" he yelled back.

"The Moon," said the girl. "It will never be yours."

So the boy set about trying to get the Moon for himself. He went to his dad.

“Dad, I want the Moon. Please get it for me.”

At first the King tried to explain that the Moon was not his to give, but the boy insisted. So the King told his wisest men that they would have to get the Moon somehow.

The wise men came up with a plan to build a tall tower all the way up to the Moon.

“When the tower is complete, the boy can go up it and grab the Moon for himself,” they explained.

It took ten years for the tower to be finished. When it was finished, the boy (who was by now a young man) was far from grateful.

"You made me wait a long time," he complained as he clambered up the steps.

The King and the boy made everyone in the kingdom come with them up the tower. Only the girl and her family did not go with them. They waited at the bottom, looking up.

Many hours of clambering later, the King, the boy, and all of their followers got to the top of the tower. The King reached out to touch the Moon first.

"Ouch!" he yelped. "The Moon is boiling hot! Do not touch it."

But the boy did not listen. He reached out and grabbed handfuls of rocks.

"Argh!" he yelled, and he dropped the red-hot rocks onto the tower.

Flames spread quickly down the wooden tower.

The wooden tower was about to collapse. The King, the boy, and all of their followers started to panic. Meanwhile, up in the sky, the African gods looked on.

“We should help those fools,” said the African gods. “They should not have tried to get the Moon for themselves, but they do not need to die.”

So the gods turned everyone on the burning tower into a bird, so that they could fly down to the ground safely.

The girl saw all of the birds flying down from the burning tower. The gods had saved them from falling, but punished them for their foolishness at the same time. From that day on, the girl told the story of the boy who wanted the Moon to anyone who would listen.